j 818.602
K849f

DETROIT PUBLIC LIBRARY
P9-BZN-293

the fairly OddParents!
NICKELODEON

FAIRLY
ODD
JOKES

KN

Based on the TV show *The Fairly OddParents™* created by Butch Hartman as seen on Nickelodeon®

SIMON SPOTLIGHT
An imprint of Simon & Schuster Children's Publishing Division
1230 Avenue of the Americas, New York, New York 10020

Manufactured in the United States of America

First Edition
2 4 6 8 10 9 7 5 3 1

ISBN 0-689-86319-5

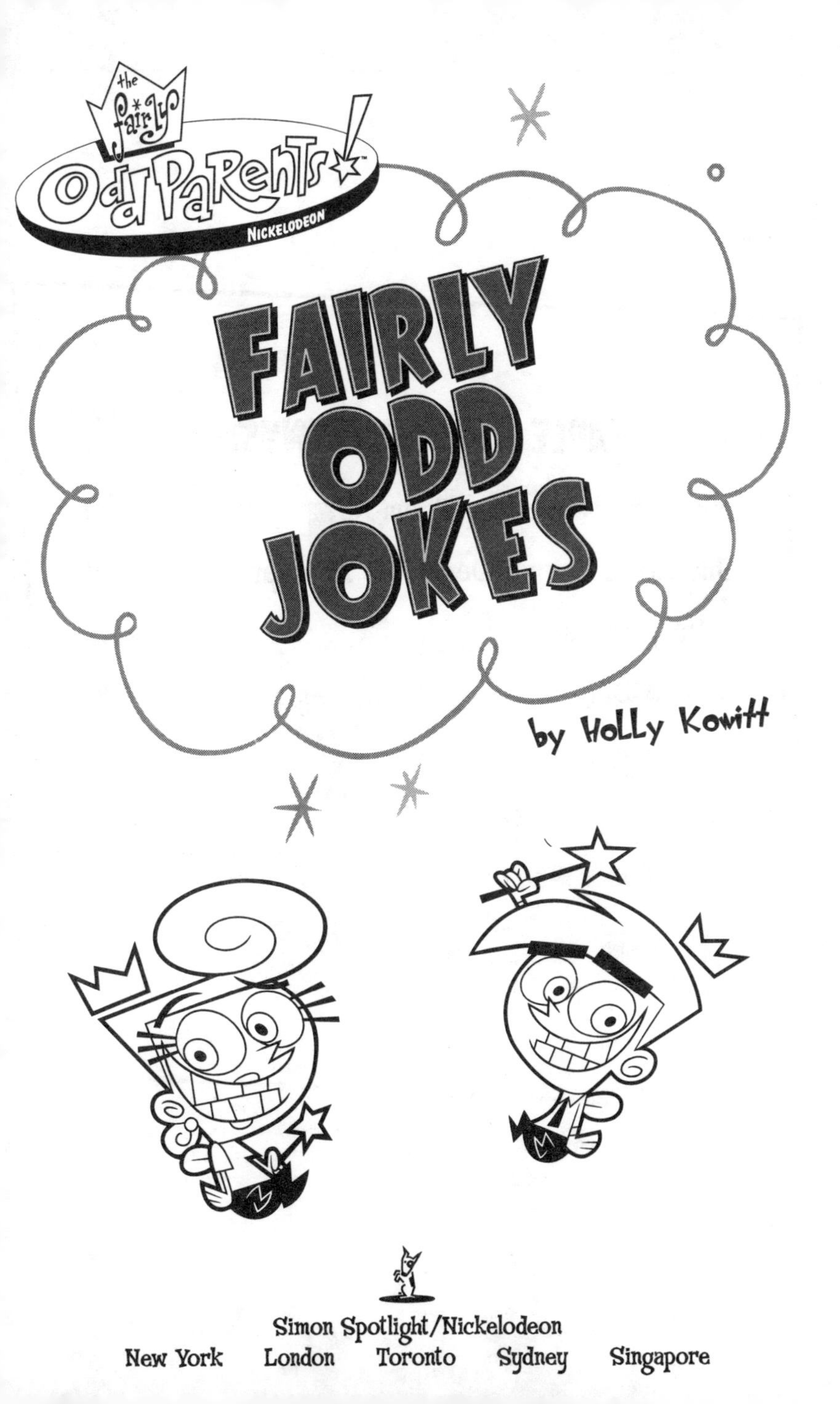
the fairly OddParents!
Nickelodeon
FAIRLY ODD JOKES
by Holly Kowitt
Simon Spotlight/Nickelodeon
New York London Toronto Sydney Singapore

TABLE OF CONTENTS

WHO'S THE FAIRIEST OF THEM ALL?

What do you call someone who can turn herself into a werewolf with the wave of her wand?
A hairy godmother.

What do you call someone who grants wishes and goes "Moo, moo"?
A dairy godmother.

ZAP!
GONE!
ZAP!
What do you call Wanda
on Halloween?
A scary godmother.

How do fairies call one another?
They use spell phones.
What did Wanda wear when
she got married?
A wedding wing.

What's Cosmo's favorite amusement park ride?
The fairy-go-round.
Why would Cosmo and Wanda make good balloons?
Because there's air in every fairy.

Which state has the most fairies?
Wish-consin.

Why did Cosmo dye the Easter Bunny green?
Because he really likes green hare.

What do fairies catch a lot of when they play baseball?
Fly balls.

POOF!

Why did Wanda change Cosmo into a clock?
She wanted to see *time* fly.

Why does Jorgen von Strangle
like visiting the dentist?
Because he knows all the drills.
What cheese do they
serve at the Fairy
Academy?
Jorgen-zola!
Who has the largest furniture
in Fairy World?
Jorgen—he's got a big chest!
POP!

What seafood does
Jorgen like best?
Mussels.
What kind of stories
does Jorgen tell?
Tall tales.

Who grants wishes to young fishermen?
Fairy CodParents.

What do all fairy movies have?
A zappy ending.

Why couldn't the lawyer win a case in Fairy Court?
He didn't have any poof!

When Cosmo turns into a dog, what does he wag?
His fairy tail.
POOF!

What do you call Timmy's
godmother when she turns
into a superhero?
Wanda Woman.
How do fairies
improve their TV
reception?
With a satellite wish.

POOF!
Why did Cosmo get a job on Wall Street?
So he could trade stocks and wands.
What do Wanda and Cosmo like best about New York?
The Staten Island Fairy.

ONE GOOD TURNER DESERVES ANOTHER

Why did Timmy lose friends when he became invisible?
Everyone could see right through him.

What does a wand do at a football game?
The wave.

Did you hear about the fairy that
became a film director?
She really made movie magic.
What does a fairy teacher
use to correct tests?
A magic marker.

What sign do Cosmo and Wanda leave on their door when they vacation at Fairy Lake?
Gone Wishin'!
POOF!
Why is Wanda a good teacher?
She takes students under her wing.

What's the fairies' motto?
"If at once you don't succeed, fly, fly again."

What do you get when Cosmo
rides a roller coaster?
Fairy whirled.
What do fairies give on
Valentine's Day?
Hugs and wishes.

Why do fairies go to the dentist?
To get their teeth crowned.

What do you have when Cosmo and Wanda wear mink coats?
Furry GodParents.

Who grants wishes to young trumpets?
The Toot Fairy.

What do you get when Wanda zaps cars to match Timmy's hat?
A pink car-nation.

How do you catch a fairy?
By the fairy tale.

What sign hangs in all of the restaurant bathrooms in Fairy World?
"Employees Must Wash Wings Before Returning to Work"

TOTALLY JAW-SOME!

Why did the Crimson Chin arrest a belt?
It held up a pair of pants.

KA-CHIN!

Why did the Bronze Knee Cap want to become a great actor?
So he could steal the show.

How does the Chin know when a villain has gone bad?
He checks his expiration date.

What's the difference between the Chin and a freezer?

One upholds justice, the other holds just ice.

POP!

What's the Crimson Chin's favorite side dish?
Masked potatoes.

KA-CHIN!

What does the Chin use to catch criminals?
The long arm of the jaw.

POP!

What's the best way to talk to the Chin?
Man-to-mandible.

Who fights for truth, justice, and the safety of leg bones everywhere? *The Crimson Shin.*

Why did Cleft, the Boy Chin Wonder, fight the Bronze Kneecap and Spatula Woman?
Because they kept trying to break the jaw.

What is Timmy's comic
book hero's favorite form
of exercise?
Chin-ups.

What happened to the Boy Chin Wonder when the Crimson Chin ran on ahead?
He was Cleft behind.

What is the Chin's favorite kind of cookie?
Crimson Chip.

What did the Crimson Chin
say to the shirt?
"You're under a vest!"
What does the Bronze Knee Cap
say on his answering machine?
"Leave a message at the sound
of the creep."

What do you get when Spatula Woman falls into a cement mixer?
A hardened criminal.

SPACED OUT

How do you learn to be a space hero?
Take a Crash course.

What does Crash Nebula call a killer potato?
His starch-enemy.

What do you get when a killer potato stomps on Timmy's favorite space hero?
Mash Nebula.

Why did Crash Nebula
cancel his ice show?
He got cold feet.
What do you call a
space hero with
poison ivy?
Rash Nebula.
What do you call a
space hero who falls
into a pool?
Splash Nebula.

What did Mark, the alien prince, say to the book?
"Take me to your reader!"

What does Mark, the alien prince, watch every year on TV?
The Out-of-This-World Series.

Why did Vicky hand Timmy over to the school bullies?
She wanted everyone to have a Turner.

TORTURING TIMMY TURNER

Timmy: *"Why'd you tell everyone that I'm a twerp?"*
Vicky: *"I didn't know it was supposed to be a secret!"*

What's Vicky's favorite day of the week?
Mean-day.

What is Vicky's favorite book?
How to Get Rich Baby-sitting by
Robin D. Turners.
What did Timmy yell to his mom when
Vicky called?
"The phony's for you."

Why did Francis bring a
hammer to the library?
The teacher *told him to hit*
the books.
What happened when Doidle ate
Chip Skylark's picture?
Vicky nearly hit the woof!

If Francis were a dog, what kind would he be?
A bully dog.

How does Francis like his steak?
Tough!

What did Francis serve at the school dance?
Punch!

Why is Timmy afraid of swamps?
Because they have Crocker-diles.

What is Timmy's teacher's favorite snack?
Cheese and Crockers.

Why does Timmy have to watch out for Mr. Crocker?
He's fairy suspicious!

What do you call a fairy-hunting squid?
A Crock-topus.

FAIRLY ODD FRIENDS

Why doesn't A.J. spend any mone
He's saving for a brainy day.

What does Timmy's scout leader order with his hamburger?
Squirrelly fries.

Why did Timmy's friend tell him a big secret?
He wanted to get it off his Chester.

Why do A.J.'s friends always
wear sunglasses around him?
Because he's so bright!
Where does A.J. soak
after a long hard day?
In a math tub.

What snack does Timmy's
friend roast over an open fire?
Chester-nuts.
How does Trixie Tang stay cool?
She has plenty of fans!
How is Trixie like
the Grand Canyon?
Both are gorges.

What kind of underwear
does Chet Ubetcha wear?
News briefs!
Why did Chet take a
job on a ship?
*He wanted to be an
anchor man.*
What happened when Chet
broke his leg?
He ended up in a news cast.

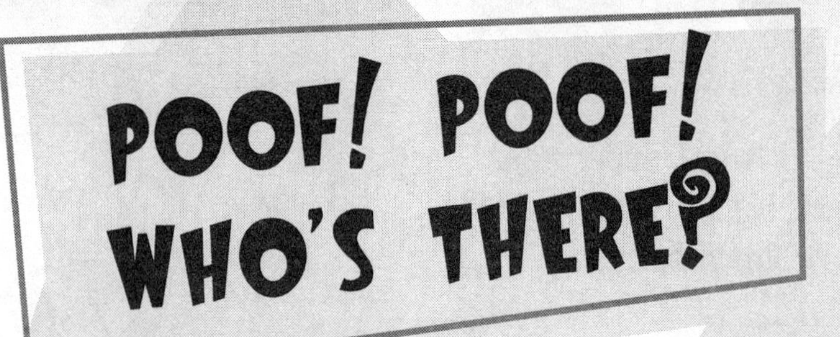

Knock-knock.
Who's there?
Cosmo.
Cosmo who?
You Cosmo trouble than any fairy I know!

Knock-knock.
Who's there?
Wanda.
Wanda who?
Wanda where Timmy went.

Knock-knock.
Who's there?
Wish.
Wish who?
Wish you would quit knocking!
Knock-knock.
Who's there?
Eve.
Eve who?
Eve-il baby-sitter here
to ruin your day.

POOF!
The End.
POOF!